On the Line

PAUL DEMKO

MAY _ 2017

Originally published as *Match Point*
by Robin Cruise

Revision Editor: Steve Shea
Cover Illustration: Andrew Bock/Beehive
Cover Design: Lucy Nielsen

International Standard Book Number:
978-1-57128-683-3

21 20 19 18 17 16 15 14 13 12
10 09 08 07 06 05 04 03 02 01

www.HighNoonBooks.com

Sports set order # 8678-9

Contents

Chapter 1

Time to Choose

Why won't she leave? My clock reads 7:35, and the summer heat is already roasting me alive in my room. Mom usually leaves for work by now. I think she's waiting for me.

I thought I could beat her this year. No soccer camp. No volleyball camp. *Definitely* no field hockey camp. Biking I could handle, but not biking *camp*.

Sports are not my thing. I know this. My friends know this. Dad knew it. Why doesn't Mom? I just want to get a part-time job at the mall, hang out with my friends, you know? But no, that's not in Mom's plans.

"Jazmine! Hurry down now. I need to talk to you before I go to work!"

This is it, I think. *She's got me.*

I take a deep breath on my way downstairs. The cooler air in the dining room calms my nerves.

"There you are, Jaz," Mom says with a smile. "Today's the last day to sign up for Youth Club sports camps, and you still haven't chosen one."

I slump down in a chair. "Do I have to, Mom? I'm not really into sports, you know, since ..."

"Honey, eighth grade was two years ago, and the PE teacher apologized!"

"He made the whole class stand around and watch me miss the basket, over and over!" I wail.

Mom sighs. Why can't she see how miserable sports make me?

"Maybe basketball isn't your sport, but your father played minor league baseball," Mom tells me, like I haven't heard this before. "Your aunt runs marathons, and Grandma swims a mile every morning. With so many great athletes in the family, I'm sure it's just a matter of time before we find the right one for you."

It doesn't help that my brother Cordell's room is like a shrine to his innocent childhood, full of football, basketball, and baseball trophies. I haven't been in there in months—nobody has—and I still feel the weight of all of that gleaming metal.

So, what's my deal? Am I ever going to be good at anything?

"Now," Mom says, dropping the catalog on the table like a sack of bricks, "what's it going to be this summer, Jazmine? Look, they have swimming and volleyball. Karate. And gymnastics!"

"Mom, I've done them all," I sigh. "You know I'm a lousy swimmer—I can barely float. I'm a failure at gymnastics. I can't even do a cartwheel. And I don't like volleyball because it hurts my wrists. Can't we just skip it this summer? Blanca doesn't do sports. And besides, how are you going to pay for it?"

This is where I get super clever. Mom has been struggling to make ends meet since Dad left. I move in for the kill. "I was thinking I could get a part time job at the mall, maybe help out with some of the bills ..."

But Mom sees right through it. "Those jobs are long gone. Adults who got laid off are taking those jobs from teenagers, and you know it. Besides, if you go near a mall, you spend all the money you have, and then some. Jazmine, you're not Blanca, and I know you remember our deal: you can hang out with your friends on the weekends, but during the week, I need to know you're keeping out of trouble. And a little exercise and fresh air never hurt anybody."

I listen to her talk for long enough to eat some cereal and rinse out my bowl.

"OK, Mom! OK!" I snap. I don't really mean to, but she is so persistent. "Just give me the catalog and I'll choose."

Mom pushes the catalog across the

table to me. I close my eyes and flip to a random page, put my finger on it and open my eyes.

"Tennis?" I guess it's no worse than the rest, but I'm no good at tennis either. What a pain.

"That's great, Jasmine. Tennis is good exercise, and I don't think you've ever tried it. I'll sign you up today. Three weeks of tennis lessons. It's five days a week, morning and afternoon, and it's not very expensive. After those three weeks, we'll see about maybe taking a little vacation."

I can't believe it. Tennis. Three weeks. And Mom thinks this is great.

After she leaves for work, I go to the living room and watch TV. I don't even see what's on. In my mind, I'm watching myself swing at the ball and miss, over and over.

Chapter 2

On the Court

Mom is so happy on Monday morning, I can't stand it. She's humming while she gets ready for work. She even packs me a sandwich—a good one, cream cheese and tomatoes—like it's some kind of special thing for me to go to stupid tennis camp and make a fool of myself.

She hands me a racket and a backpack with my lunch inside. "Use this racket, Jaz, and make sure not to break it or lose it. Your father may come back some day for it."

She'll probably dent it against his head, but OK, I think.

I look closely at it. My hand barely fits around the worn grip, but the frame is smooth, like new almost. I tap the strings. *They're so tight—is that a good thing?* I wonder.

After breakfast, I grab a bottle of water and my bike helmet and I'm out the door before Mom can call after me to be careful. It's not like she needs to worry. Our street ends at the river, and the bike path runs along it, staying out of most of the bad parts of town. Just past my school (Go, Panthers!), I turn east to ride to the Youth Club. I hardly have to ride in any traffic.

I get there ten minutes early, lock my bike, and check in at the front desk. The clerk makes a mark next to my name on a list, and tells me where to go. I walk around under the warm sun until I find the tennis courts.

There are four of them, empty of people. There are a bunch of wire baskets holding tennis balls over to one side. It's getting really hot out here, and it's not even 9 a.m. I'm heading for a bit of shade when two nervous, black-haired boys who almost look like twins come in together and quietly begin stretching. They're dressed almost the same, have the same haircut, and seem to know what they're doing. I'm just thinking, *Great—probably everyone is some suburban jock. I bet it's all boys, too*—when in walks another one. He's tall, and looks kind of familiar. Two other boys come in after him. They crouch down in some shade and whisper to each other, maybe in Spanish, but I can't really hear.

Next, two girls my age come through the gate and drop their sports bags on the court. They take up a bench big enough for four people and just sit there glaring. One is checking her hair extensions while the other seems to be keeping an eye on everyone. Everything about them says, *Don't get in my way.*

I'm just about ready to give up on the whole class when I hear a familiar voice.

"Jaz!"

I can't believe it. It's Blanca! She

hustles across the court and gives me one of her back-breaking hugs.

"You got a perm and painted your nails to play tennis?" I tease her. Her hair and nails are always perfect, but today she's also wearing baggy sweatpants, despite the heat. Blanca is as worried about her legs as I am about my failure at sports.

"My mom made me sign up. My doctor told her I need to get exercise, but it's going to be cool if you're here, too!" Blanca said. "I can't believe my mom, though, she—"

A short, blonde-haired woman with muscular legs comes through the gate, and Blanca turns to look at her. I know she's thinking, *Is this old woman our coach?* The woman is wearing a bright blue Youth Club t-shirt, sun visor and yellow shorts, and carrying a racket. She starts talking in a loud voice.

"Hi, everybody!" the woman says with a wave. "My name is Amanda, and

I'm really excited to be your teacher. All kinds of people can be really great tennis players, and I'm here to help you start, or at least to have some fun with it!"

I look around and see most of the students are staring at Amanda. *She sure is loud.* Before we know what's happening, she has us lining up with our backs to the fence. I'm almost at the end, trying to hide behind the tall guy. Blanca is hiding behind me.

"This," Amanda says, sweeping her racket along a white line in front of us, "is the baseline. You can think of it as home base, because most of the time this is where you want to be."

Amanda looks at me and I freeze. *Don't start at this end. I hate sports.* I breathe a sigh of relief when she turns away and calls out to the almost-twins, "Let's start with you two."

Chapter 3

Forehand

I watch her talk with one of them, position him, and bounce a tennis ball in front of him. He swings the racket, and the ball makes a popping sound off the racket's strings. It flies low and fast over the net, bounces in the court, and hits the fence behind it.

Wow, I think, *he's pretty good.*

And then his brother hits it exactly the same. I guess they were nervous about something besides tennis.

Amanda gets closer and closer, working her way down the line. She talks to each student before bouncing a ball. The student swings the racket, there's a popping sound, and the ball goes over the net and hits the fence behind the court.

My stomach feels like it's full of butterflies. I look at Blanca, who's watching every move, too. When I turn around, Amanda is talking to the tall boy next to me.

"Hi, there!" she says. "What's your name?"

"Errick," he said, "with two *R*s and a *C-K*."

"Well, Errick with two *R*s and a *C-K*," Amanda says, "have you ever played any tennis?"

Errick looks down. "A little. My dad and I used to play."

"Cool," Amanda says. "Let's see what you can do."

Amanda drops a ball in front of Errick, and I hold my breath. I watch the way he swings, his racket following through, his weight shifting onto his left foot. Somebody whistles as the ball blazes over the net, barely skimming it and landing a few inches inside the baseline on the other side.

Amanda turns to Errick and says, "Awesome."

Now it's my turn. I'm not ready, and I don't even really hear Amanda asking me my name, I'm so nervous. She guides me by the shoulder to make me face the right way. Then the ball is bouncing, I'm swinging—and the ball is still bouncing.

I missed the ball.

"Just relax," Amanda says quietly, "and keep your eye on the ball."

This isn't eighth-grade PE, I remind myself. *I can do this.* I take a deep breath, and try to relax. The ball bounces, I keep my eye on it, and there's a popping sound.

"I hit it!" I shout, and Blanca snorts back a laugh, pointing at the tiny yellow speck of a ball flying *over* the fence and into the street.

"Whatever," I grumble. "I'm no good at sports, it's not like—" I stop when I see Amanda's face.

"Wow, Jazmine!" she says, looking happy. "You've got a lot of power there. With your height and power like that, you could be the next Serena Williams!"

I can't believe she just said that. I mean, *really*? Why not some player who *doesn't* look like me? Still, Serena Williams is the best pro tennis player I can think of, so I guess it's not so bad.

At least she's encouraging me. I feel like maybe I can do this.

I turn to watch Blanca as she takes a swing. She's left-handed, so Amanda uses her own left hand to show Blanca how to hit the ball. Blanca is awkward at first, but Amanda helps her stand the right way. Then Amanda bounces the ball, Blanca swings, and even though the ball smacks into the net, her face opens into a smile.

"Great start, Blanca! Just a little higher, and you'll get it," Amanda says.

Blanca looks so goofy and happy right now, that I can't help but smile, too. But then she sees me grinning, and her smile vanishes. Weird.

Amanda finishes up with Blanca and then jogs out in front of us again, halfway to the net.

"You kids did great!" she exclaims. I look down the line and see everyone at least paying attention. I guess that's why Amanda is so loud.

"Now we're going to practice the basic stroke in tennis. It's called the forehand. You all just did part of one, so it's no big deal anymore. Now watch how I do the whole stroke, so you can copy me. What I want you to do is to kind of step toward the net when you swing. That gives your stroke extra power. Now, watch me."

Amanda hits three balls to show us what she means. With each swing, she shifts her weight from the right foot to the left, almost like taking a step toward the net. All three of the balls she hits bounce at exactly the same spot. This looks kind of fun.

"Ow!" I whisper, and turn to glare at Blanca. "Why did you poke me?"

Blanca points at my feet. "You're copying her!"

I didn't realize it, but Blanca is right. I'm totally copying Amanda's movements, shifting my weight and holding my racket in my right hand.

Amanda turns around and points at me. "Way to mimic me, Jazmine. You've got plenty of power, so if you can get the forehand swing just right, you'll be hard to beat."

That got my attention. *Me? Hard to beat?* I make a funny face at Blanca, hoping for a little laugh like usual, but she shakes her head at me and looks away.

Chapter 4

The Sweet Spot

When Amanda splits the class up into pairs to practice, I am stunned to see Blanca pair up with one of the tough girls. I think it was the lookout. Her friend is probably fixing her hair in the bathroom.

I find myself standing next to the tall guy. He asks, "You have a partner yet?"

"No," I say. I don't know what's up with Blanca, but it can't hurt to practice with Errick.

"Alright then," Errick says. "You can hit first." He jogs to the other side of the court. I know I've seen him before, maybe at school.

I can't think about that now. Amanda is looking right at me. I take a deep breath, bounce the ball the way Amanda had shown us, and swing.

The ball bounces near his feet and hits the metal fence behind him. "Go ahead and do all of yours. I'll go next." Before I know what I am doing, I hit three balls in a row, each one bouncing just about right.

One of the almost-twins is just to my right. He looks like he knows what he's doing, so I stand like he does. Maybe I'll look like I know what I'm doing, too.

When Errick does hit the ball, it races past me so fast, I can feel the breeze. Two more balls come past me, and I realize I've been staring, so I look away.

We play for a few more minutes, and then take a water break. It's really hot already, but there's a bucket of ice with bottled water in it. I grab two, and head over to talk to Blanca. I *need* to talk to her, so I drag her by the hand to a bench where there's a little shade.

"What's with you?" Blanca demands. She is sweating from the heat and exercise, but I know that's not what got to her.

I hand her a bottle. "I should ask you the same thing. Why did you have to make that face at me back there? And why didn't you want us to be partners?"

Blanca looks down, still holding the cold plastic bottle, unopened. "It's just ... when did you get like this?" she asks.

"Like ... like *what?*" I'm shocked. What is she talking about? I can't deal with her and the heat, so I open the bottle and fill my mouth with the icy water.

"Popular. Cool. Athletic." Blanca mumbles the words, still looking down. The condensation drips off her water bottle and leaves small splashes on the court surface between her feet.

What did she just say? I can't help myself. The laugh just bursts out of me, pushing the mouthful of water mostly out my nose, which only makes me laugh more. Blanca is having a hard time staying angry at me, too.

"Sorry. Never mind. I guess I thought you and I were the same. It's OK. I won't stay jealous just because you can play tennis."

Amanda interrupts before I can answer, shouting at the class that we're going to move inside the gym for a while because of the heat. I know the gym is air-conditioned, and my best friend isn't jealous of me anymore, so I figure it's all good.

In the cool of the gym, Amanda has everyone stand in a semi-circle around her. She tells us kids to put our rackets down and watch her. "I want to show you something cool about your rackets," she says.

Amanda holds her racket by the head, and swings the handle at a ball.

It bounces away in a random direction, and we all laugh.

"So, who can tell me why we don't hit the ball this way?"

The almost-twins raise their hands at the same time, then Errick does, and another boy I haven't talked to yet.

"So only the boys know this?" Amanda teases.

One of the tough-looking girls makes a really rude sound. Then Amanda looks at me and I freeze. *Does she think I did that?*

"Jazmine, why don't we hit the ball with the handle instead of the strings?" Amanda asks, looking at me intently.

"Because the ball doesn't go where you want it to?" My voice sounds so tiny, it's like an admission of guilt—but I didn't do it!

"Exactly!" Amanda says, shifting her gaze to the rest of the class. "There's a better part of the racket to hit the ball with."

She shows us a few more wrong places first: the top of the frame, the throat of the racket, her hand on the handle. The balls roll and bounce away with our laughs. "So what's left?" she asks. The class is silent, but she's not answering her own question. She knows she has to keep us interested, and, based on the rude sound, we're not all on her side yet.

"The sweet spot." I turn to look at the voice. It's Errick, still serious and quiet, like he doesn't want to stand out.

"That's right," says Amanda. "Point to the sweet spot on your racket, Errick, and show everyone."

Some of the kids are having little conversations, and Amanda ignores them. I almost feel like helping her out, but I don't want to stand out, either. I don't even know these people, and some of them look like trouble.

Chapter 5

Up to Speed

"OK, enough standing around," Amanda says. "We're going to concentrate on the two *F*s this week: forehand and fitness. You're going to practice your forehand, the way we practiced earlier, by hitting against a wall. Try hitting the ball with your sweet spot each time. In half an hour, we run."

Run? "We have to run?" I ask.

"Sure!" Amanda says in her big voice. "Tennis games can last over two hours, with only short breaks. Even when you're tired, you have to be able to sprint to get to the ball. So get used to running!"

That's OK. I can handle a little running. I look around for Blanca, and I see her really concentrating. The ball keeps going all over the place, but she really works at it.

After a while, Amanda calls us all in. We leave the balls in a bin, and set our rackets down next to it.

"OK, that was forehand, now for the fitness. I'll show you the drill," she calls out. She starts at the end line of the basketball court, then sprints to a line about 20 feet away. She touches the line with her hand, then sidesteps back to the end line. Every time she turns, she touches the line with her hand. She sprints to half court, and I'm thinking, *What, there's more?* She does the sidestep back again, then jogs all the way to the other end of the court, not going super fast, and sprints back to where she started.

"Everyone take it slow the first time, so I can remind you of what to do. Also, don't run into each other."

I'm thinking, *she isn't even out of breath*, when all of a sudden, she tells us to line up, and shouts, "Go!"

We're all over the place. I start late, and Errick sprints across the whole court. Blanca is side-stepping instead of sprinting from the beginning. We all stop when Amanda, whose laugh is about as loud as her yell, nearly falls down just from watching us. The rest of us join in, and after Amanda shows us one more time, we actually get it.

It's way harder than Amanda made it look, and we're all dripping in sweat within minutes. Amanda has us jog around the court twice, then do the sprint thing again once. Then she lets us go for lunch.

"Get lots of water. Stay out of the sun, and be back on the tennis courts in 45 minutes!"

I take out my bag lunch and look for Blanca. She looks at the paper sack and wrinkles her nose. "What, you run out of spending money again? I'm going to the café!"

If anyone else said that to me, I would take it as an insult. I look around and see a couple of the other kids laughing. But it's not a joke to me. It's a challenge.

Blanca heads off to the café, and I am right on her heels. "You know, *my* lunch is nutritious!" I say to my friend's back. Man, she is fast when she wants to be. I'm jogging to keep up! But she doesn't answer.

"Don't even think about anything fried!" I tell her.

She turns around and stares me down. "Don't you start with me, Jaz. I get credit for working out. Now I have to eat!"

There's a line of people waiting to order at the café counter. Blanca calms down a bit, and says, "I know what you're trying to do, but don't you see how hard it is for me?" She looks up at me, then down at her baggy sweatpants. *Wait, is she crying?*

"Hey, Blanca," I start, but she cuts me off.

"Don't worry, I'm not going to eat a burger and fries. My mom called the café and told them not to let me eat bad foods." She's not crying, but it's taking all her effort.

Wow, that's rough, I think. When we get to the front of the line, Blanca places her order. When it's ready, we go sit down in the shade outside the café. I don't say a word about her salad, and she doesn't tease me about my cream cheese and tomato sandwich. Actually, for once, she looks like she wants a bite.

We've gone over the math of her diet again and again. We know what she can eat, and what she can't. I'm actually kind of proud of her. She finishes her salad, checks her watch, and says it's time to go back to the tennis courts. Blanca's my friend. I know she really wants to fit in, and she hates being judged for how she looks.

We stop by the gym to get our rackets. I see a tall boy sitting on a bench in the hallway, writing in a notebook and chewing on his fingernails. It's Errick. I wonder what he's doing, when Amanda walks out of an office. She says, "OK, everyone, lunch is over! Let's get in some tennis before the day's over!"

Blanca and I head out before Errick can get his stuff together.

Chapter 6

The Partner

The afternoon goes by quickly. I get to play tennis with just about everyone. Raúl and Edgar don't talk much, but they're great athletes, and Edgar smiles a lot. Ta'Nara, the girl with extensions, actually knows how to play tennis. Her friend MiShaun is about like me. Well, she's as bad at tennis as I am. In other ways, she's totally different, like all the tattoos, and the fact that she only talks to Ta'Nara.

The almost-twins, Matt and Connor, are really good players, when they're not distracted by Ta'Nara and MiShaun's hostile attitude. Anyway, I feel good, so I'm nice to them, and they show me tons of tricks. I find out they go to a private school a few miles away.

That night, after biking home, I'm totally sore. Blanca texts me a bunch of times.

i h8 running, so tired
ur tv show is on, i bet i kno whats gonna happen
salad 4 dinner 2, sucks 2b me

I have enough time to shower and maybe watch some TV, but yawning every ten seconds is really bugging me. I say good night to my mom, who for once stays up later than me, and it's off to Dreamland.

When I wake up, I feel terrible. My legs are killing me! Even my arms hurt when I walk, so I try to step softly. I tell my mom I need a doctor, and she laughs.

"Honey, that's just sore muscles. You'll get used to it. I left you money for lunch. It's on the counter." And then she's out the door. *Fine. Be like that.*

I eat some cereal for breakfast, being

careful not to pull any more muscles while I'm eating. I wonder if Blanca is OK. Things are still tough for her, but not as bad as when we first met, two years ago. Back then, we were both freshmen, and bad at making friends. On the first day of school, we both chose seats near the back of class. And when everyone else was noisy with the start of a new school year, we were quiet.

I remember not wanting to talk to her. She was wearing all black clothes, too tight. And she had way too much makeup on. I didn't know what kind of gang dressed like that, and I didn't want to.

For my part, I was wearing my dad's old, green sweater. He had left it behind after the last fight with my mom.

Blanca and I were the absolute worst-dressed kids in the class. Of course everybody else avoided us. In the end, we only had each other to talk to.

My cereal this morning (whole grains, no sugar, of course) makes me think of Blanca. I got on her case about eating healthy foods and all that. She had these heavy, fried lunches, and all sorts of junk food and giant sodas all the time. She saw me eating my sandwiches and fruit every day.

As far back as I can remember, my brother and I ate broccoli and spinach like an army of rabbits. It was something my parents agreed on, one of the few things. My brother got strong, like our parents. For me, I'm no athlete, but I almost never catch a cold, and I never thought about dieting till I met Blanca. She, on the other hand, had never seen anyone eat what I ate.

"Do you want some of mine?" Blanca asked me at lunch one day, not long after the school year started.

I had to tell her that I liked my lunches, and I liked how they made me feel. I still remember how she looked down at herself, her second deluxe hamburger still in hand, and stopped talking to me for the rest of the day. Since I was the only one she would talk to, she had a pretty quiet day.

The next day at lunch, Blanca had a small sandwich on whole wheat bread, and some carrots instead of french fries. I didn't say a thing. We just ate our lunches.

You have to hand it to Blanca. She was miserable, but she was determined. And after a few days, I felt I could talk to her about it.

"You like carrots now, huh?" I tried to sound relaxed.

She smiled and said, "I hate them. They don't taste like anything, and I'm always hungry."

I looked at her and saw me, but with different problems. *My* problems started when my family fell apart. My brother was in serious trouble, and my parents argued all the time. They had been arguing for years. In middle school, I used to tell them I was going to a friend's house, but I never did. Out on the streets, I thought I was tough for a little while. Then I saw how things really were, and I almost got in more trouble than I could handle. By that time, Dad had gone, Cordell too, and it was just me and Mom.

When I first met her, Blanca looked trapped. I thought about how, before he got caught up in things, Cordell used to protect me. He would always take me to movies and cool places to hang out when Mom and Dad got into their fights. I wondered if Blanca had anyone like Cordell.

"Do you have any brothers or sisters?" I asked her.

"I'm the oldest," Blanca said, then counted off on her fingers. "I have a sister in seventh grade, a brother in fifth, and another brother in third."

"Let's hang out this weekend," I

said. The look on her face, well, I must have looked like that to Cordell, back in the day.

The first week of tennis camp goes by super-fast. The two best things are, first, I find out I like tennis, and second, Blanca stops wearing her baggy sweats.

"It's too hot, Jaz. I can't sweat buckets just to hide my legs," she says.

That was Wednesday, and she gets more serious about tennis every day. She's still terrible, but she doesn't seem to care, laughing and chasing after the balls that fly off her racket in all directions.

Two best things are good, but there's a *not*-best thing, too. I'm not like Blanca—I *care* if I don't play well. And I've got a problem. I mean, I'm getting the hang of this forehand business. Amanda is already teaching us the backhand, and that's going better than I thought. Even my serve is coming on. The thing I'm no good at is getting to the ball. I mean, if someone hits it right to me, I can handle it. But if someone hits it away from me—which is what people try to do in tennis games!—I can't figure out where it's going to land. So half the time I'm not there. It's weird, I know.

There's not much time to worry about this. I'm exhausted every night, barely managing a shower, dinner, and a half hour of TV or whatever before passing out.

On Friday, though, Amanda announces that we will have a tournament on Thursday and Friday, the week after next.

"A doubles tournament," Amanda adds. *Great. Now I have to drag someone else down.*

"No way, Jaz. I am *not* going to be your partner." Blanca turns me down, cold.

"But why? You can't just abandon me!" I honestly don't know who else could stand to play with me. It's Saturday evening, and I can't think of anyone else I'd want to practice with, which is all we're doing for three days before the tournament.

"You aren't good enough to help me, girlfriend."

I can't believe Blanca's saying that to me!

"And I'm not good enough to help *you*, either," she adds. Then she tells me what she's up to.

"I asked Connor to be my partner. Amanda told him he couldn't team up with his brother. He's nice, and I think I can learn from him."

"Wait," I say, trying to understand. "You want to learn about *tennis*?"

"Yes, I do," she says in a serious

37

tone. "And you're just about out of time. Connor's brother Matt already got snapped up by Ta'Nara. I heard her bragging about how she's going to win the tournament."

I imagine Ta'Nara, with her tough look and long, blonde extensions, cornering Matt and forcing him to partner up, and I laugh. But still, who's left for me? MiShaun—no way. Maybe one of those two guys who mostly speak Spanish. I think the taller one is Edgar.

Chapter 7

Practice

On Sunday morning, I leave before Mom is even awake and practice hitting against a wall at the park. I spend a lot of time chasing balls. When I get back, she asks me what's wrong.

"Nothing," I say, louder than I mean to. *How can she tell?*

Mom sighs. She tries again. "You know, honey, I'm proud of you."

I don't expect this, so I take off my tennis shoes without saying a word.

"You didn't want to try anything. You were scared. And now look at you." Her eyes go from my tennis bag to the sweat dripping from my face. "You take this seriously."

"I just don't like to lose, is all."

Mom smiles. "That used to stop you.

Now it gets you going. Just do your best, honey, and don't worry about losing. If you try hard enough, no matter what the score, you never really lose."

I think about it on the way to tennis camp Monday morning. When I get there, the court gate is still locked. I check my watch and realize I'm 20 minutes early. *Did I ride that fast?*

Looking for something to do, I check out the gym. I have some tennis balls and my racket with me, so I try to hit against the wall in the basketball court, like we did the first day.

Who should I ask to be my partner in the tournament? I run through the list for the 100th time in my mind. Edgar? Raúl? Errick? I can't think and hit against the wall at the same time, apparently. Either that or the wall just isn't hitting it back to me! The ball keeps getting away, and then I hear this quiet laugh. I turn my head and see Errick.

OK. Raúl, then. I throw the ball at Errick, hard.

"Don't be mad," he yells, dodging the ball. "I just heard you practicing, and when I came in, you were all focused, and you kept missing ..."

I turn away and stuff my dad's racket into my backpack, then brush past Errick without saying anything. He can laugh. I don't care.

The court is open now and full of people practicing tennis. In the first week of camp, only a few of us knew how to hit a ball, and now I see Blanca stretching and talking happily with Connor, and Matt and Ta'Nara already practicing with each other. *Wow. That's fast.*

Amanda jogs through the gate and starts up class with her usual energy. We must be getting used to her. Nobody looks startled by her anymore.

I see Errick looking at me. He's holding the tennis ball I left in the gym. I head the other way and stand next to

Blanca, who grins at me. *What's she so happy about?*

"Today we start practicing in teams for the tournament," Amanda announces. "I see lots of partners already. I need one person from each team to sign up for the two of you. Then I can make a schedule. Let's get that done now. The rest of you stretch a bit. And drink some water! It's going to be another hot day!"

I hang back as just about everyone else runs around. Amanda is signing people up and wishing them good luck. Raúl and Edgar are adjusting the strings on Edgar's racket. Connor makes a joke I can't hear. Blanca laughs, and Connor blushes. Ta'Nara hits Matt's shoulder, but she smiles, too.

After a while, I realize Amanda is looking at me, and then at Errick. "Well, which one of you is going to sign up?" She laughs. "Never mind. You two are going to be *awesome!*"

I'm thinking, *How did I get stuck with this guy?* when Errick clears his throat. He walks over to Amanda and talks to her in a voice I can't quite hear. He looks smaller, somehow, and I can see Amanda looking concerned.

"Well, that's pretty tough, Errick. Maybe you should rely on your tournament partner for help, though."

Errick looks quickly at me, then back at Amanda, and shakes his head. *What are they talking about? Am I that bad?*

Amanda puts a hand on Errick's shoulder and tells him, "Try your best." Then she gets up and starts to direct the class. It's backhand, today, and I need to concentrate to get anywhere with it.

We practice all morning, and then at lunch, Blanca happily drags me to the café. She gets halfway through her salad before she puts down her fork and frowns at me.

"What's wrong?"

See, that's the thing about having

43

a friend. You try to be there for her, and then when you don't even know you need it, she's there for you. Unfortunately, I'm still kind of new to the concept, so I start talking, and can't really stop.

I tell Blanca about everything. *I practiced against the wall, and the balls kept getting past me. I rode to the Club in half the time today. I'm happy I get to hang out with you. My mom keeps looking at me funny. I wonder if my brother misses his trophies. Errick's a jerk for laughing at me when I practiced. And now I'm stuck with him as a partner. But what was he saying to Amanda?*

She smiles at me. "Is that it? That's nothing! You should try doing all that with an extra 50 pounds on you. And I'm not even as tall as you!"

I guess I'm just realizing my friend only *looks like* she's in control.

I know what Blanca's going to say, so I say it for her. "OK, OK. I'll get over myself. But what do you think I should do?"

"Do? Play tennis! It's perfect! You'll play better, get stronger, hang out with your best friend, keep your mom happy, get your own trophy, make Errick stop laughing at you, and maybe even figure out what's wrong with him. See? Perfect." Blanca folds her arms and looks at me as if she solved all my problems.

Then I think, *well, maybe she's right.* So I do what she says.

Chapter 8

Finding Out

By lunchtime Wednesday, I'm hitting backhand, serving OK, and having a good time. I still let too many balls get by. But I have a bigger problem on my mind.

When everyone else sits down with their bag lunches or heads off to the café, I follow Amanda into the main building, by the registration desk. She's about to go through a door marked "EMPLOYEES ONLY" when I call out to her.

She stops. "Yes, Jazmine?" The door is half-open. I bet she wants to eat lunch.

"Uh, Amanda, I ..." I start, and then realize I don't know quite how to ask this. *Why didn't I think this through?*

Amanda gets it already. Maybe I

46

don't give her enough credit. "Is it about Errick? Did you talk to him? So he can play with you, right?" she asks.

"Wait, what?" I'm confused.

Now Amanda looks concerned again, like on Monday.

"You don't know."

It's not a question. Amanda checks her watch, then says, "Come with me. And be quiet."

I follow—not sure why. We go in the gym through the side door. It's a little office, and there, in a small room with a few computers and study desks, is Errick. He is too tall for the furniture, and he's frowning with concentration. We sneak out.

"I don't get it." I admit.

Amanda looks at her watch again. "Well, do you want to play in the tournament, or not?"

I'm confused again. "What's that got to do with Errick studying?"

"I can't tell you. You have to ask

him. And don't say you found out anything from me. Just ..." Amanda has that concerned look again. "Just do it today. Tomorrow might be too late."

Why should I care about Errick's problems? Don't I have enough? But, wait. At least I have Blanca. I don't think Errick has any friends here.

We spend the afternoon hitting balls with our doubles partners. I can tell Errick isn't smiling, even when I don't see his face. His body language says it all. And his tennis game stinks. That's weird. But it's OK, because it gives me an idea. The chance to use it comes when we're picking up tennis balls at the net.

"Hey! You're gonna need to practice some more if we're on the same team. That last serve of mine was nothing, and you just hit it into the net."

"What?" he asks. He's so distracted he has no idea what I said.

"You got something on your mind?" I ask. "If you play like this in the tournament, we're never gonna make it."

Errick looks away. "I'm sorry. I might not play in the tournament at all."

"What?" Now it's my turn to ask this question, only I do it loudly. "What do you mean?"

Errick motions for me to follow him to the water fountain. Amanda sees us, and fans herself with her hand, as if to say she knows how hot we must be.

After we drink, Errick looks at his feet and says, "I have a test coming up, and if I don't pass it, my dad won't let me play in the tournament."

I start to ask when the test is, but he interrupts.

"*And* I would have to take the class again."

Ouch, that bad? "So that's why you're never around. Where do you go?"

"Advance Tutor Center, down on 18th Street."

"What subject?"

Errick looks at me like he really doesn't want to say, but then he mumbles, "algebra."

My smile makes him frown. "Don't laugh at me," he says. "I'm already a year behind. This could mess up my graduation."

I talk fast, so he gets rid of the idea that I'm making fun of him. "I'll trade you."

He looks puzzled, so I continue. "I'm pretty good at math. I'll help you study for algebra, but I need your help with something."

He never stops smiling the whole time I explain my idea to him.

Chapter 9

Winners

Somewhere around the second set of our first tournament match, on the last Thursday of camp, I started to feel like I knew what I was doing. That was yesterday, before I scraped my knee in a fall, served into Errick's back (twice), and—*yes!*—served three aces in a row to win our final match in the afternoon.

Today, I've been on fire.

Errick and I are up against Matt and Ta'Nara, and they're really a good team. Matt's small, but a natural athlete. His serve leaves skid marks. And Ta'Nara charges the net like a demon. Errick is at least a foot taller than her, but he can't seem to get a shot past her when she plays close like that.

Still, I can't complain. We spent the

last five days, including Saturday and Sunday, huddled over algebra books and chasing balls around tennis courts. Blanca winks at me all the time, like something's going on, but I'm smiling because now I get it. I can anticipate where the balls are going to go.

See, my problem wasn't hitting the ball. Just like Amanda said, I've got power. And I've got pretty good accuracy, too. But I could never figure out the other player's ball.

Errick fixed all that. He showed me how players give clues about where they're going to hit the ball. It's in how they position themselves, the direction they face, how they strike the ball. You have to learn how to read the clues. I didn't even know there *were* clues before Errick.

Errick says it was the same for him in algebra. He was clueless, so to speak, like me in tennis. It's a good thing I'm as good a math coach as he is a tennis coach. He passed the math test Monday. OK, so he barely passed it—but now he at least passed algebra.

But today, right now, all that matters is returning Matt's serve.

Matt and Ta'Nara won the first set, 6–3. We're in the second set, and Errick and I are up 5–4. If we can just win two more points, we'll win the set. Then we'll have to play a third for the match.

Ta'Nara is serving. I watch her toss the ball up and swing her arm over in a blur. I know where the ball's going before it crosses the net, and I'm two steps away when it bounces. I stretch, connect, and return the ball so Ta'Nara has to race across the baseline to lob it back. Errick's ready at the net, and uses his height to smash an overhead. Matt can't touch it.

One more point.

Ta'Nara serves wide, to Errick's backhand. He returns it crosscourt, with a smooth motion. Matt tries to reach it at the net, but Errick's shot is too good. Ta'Nara runs it down—she's fast—and barely gets a racket on it. I move to the net and cover the middle—I know that's where the ball's coming. I'm right. I smack the ball hard between Matt and Ta'Nara. *Game and set.*

Amanda comes by to watch us during the third set. It's my serve, and I'm nervous. I want to impress Amanda with my power and accuracy. I toss the ball, swing hard—and it hits the fence without touching the ground. Lots of power, no accuracy. Ta'Nara gives me a look like *Go back to school*, and Amanda smiles.

OK, I still have my second serve. I can do this. I block the traffic sounds, the sun's heat, the burning scrape on my knee, the watching eyes of Amanda—they're all gone. Toss. Reach. Strike. Follow through.

And then Errick's grinning at me.

"Nice ace, Jaz!" he says, and gives me a high five.

Ta'Nara scowls, like she's still looking for the ball that just whizzed past her.

A second serve ace, that's rare. *Go, me!*

That's my favorite point of the third set. By the time we're halfway through the set, all the other teams have finished, and everyone is wiped out and getting silly. Errick and I lose track of who's supposed to be serving, and then we all forget the score. We're laughing and having a good time.

Amanda tells us to flip a coin to decide the winners. Matt and Ta'Nara win the coin toss, and we all cheer. We're too tired to care about the score.

It's late, the last day of camp. Matt and Connor's parents are there, waiting in their business suits to pick the boys up. Edgar waves at the almost-twins, and I do, too. Matt waves to Ta'Nara.

Blanca gives me a back-breaking

hug when her mother picks her up.

I head to the bike rack to get ready. I wave to Raúl and Edgar at the bus stop, and they shout something in Spanish that I *think* means "see you later." Probably. They're nice guys, after all.

Something's missing, I realize. I turn around and see Errick.

"Thanks," is all he says.

It's all that's needed. The three of us will see each other in a few weeks at school. Errick and I will help Blanca eat healthy. Blanca and I will help Errick with his math. And Errick and Blanca will help keep me happy. That's what friends are for, right?

If you enjoyed this book you
might also like *Outside Shot,* in the same set.
Turn the page to read a few pages of it.

Outside Shot

BY PAUL DEMKO

There's this dream I've been having, over and over since last year. I'm playing basketball, but not on some old asphalt court with bent hoops. I'm in a shiny, new arena jam-packed with fans. There are cheerleaders, and right behind the bench, my mother and my two big brothers sit in courtside seats.

It's the fourth quarter. My team is behind by 11 points, and the clock is ticking down. The coach calls our last time-out and tells us how we're going to win. He points at me. "You're the key. You can make it happen."

So we get back on the court, and

run our plays, shutting the other team's scoring down to nothing. I shoot a couple three-pointers. I get a pass right by the basket and make a slam dunk. On one play, I make a blistering, cross-court pass to our center. He scores, and then we're just one point down. With half a minute to go, the other team stalls for time, trying to drag out their one-point lead.

Then I see my chance. I get a steal, snap the ball to our point guard, and we're on a fast break. He's up against some huge guy, so he dishes the ball back to me, and I go in for a lay-up.

Suddenly, everything is in slow-motion. There's a spotlight on me, and everyone in the arena is watching me. I know I am about to win the game for us, when I hear a whistle, and then I'm standing in front of the referee. The game is stopped. The ref says, "Get off this court, kid. Don't you know you don't belong here?"

I hand the ball to the ref, and start to walk back to the bench. I look down and see I'm wearing a different uniform from all the other players on the court. Then I see that my brothers on the sideline are wearing the same uniform as me, but they're not even watching anymore. And my mom has left the arena.